Everglades Escapades

by Bobbi JG Weiss & David Cody Weiss

Illustrated by Artful Doodlers

SCHOLASTIC INC.

New York   Toronto   London   Auckland   Sydney
Mexico City   New Delhi   Hong Kong   Buenos Aires

KLaSKY
CSUPO INC.

Published by Scholastic Inc.,
90 Old Sherman Turnpike, Danbury, CT 06816.

SCHOLASTIC and associated logos are trademarks
and/or registered trademarks of Scholastic Inc.

ISBN 0-439-56285-6

First Scholastic Printing, February 2004

Chapters

"Isn't this great?" said Eliza Thornberry to her chimp pal, Darwin. "The Florida Everglades! I can't wait to meet the animals here!"

"I've already met all the bugs," Darwin grumbled, slapping at a mosquito.

Eliza hurried down inside the Commvee.
"When are we stopping?" she asked
her mother.

Marianne Thornberry cut
the engine. "Right now,"
she said. "This looks
like a good spot."

"Excellent!" said Nigel Thornberry, Eliza's father. "Time to get some footage of the Roseate Spoonbill. Beautiful bird, that. Member of the ibis family."

"And I'm going to Atlantis Park!" came an excited voice.

Eliza looked at her older sister, Debbie. "Why go to a park *about* the Everglades when you have the *real* Everglades right here?" she asked, puzzled.

"Because," said Debbie, "at a nice tidy park I can hang with other kids without ants in my hair, beetles down my pants—"

Debbie yelped as Donnie grabbed her Cheez Munchies. "Or wild creatures grabbing my food!" she finished in disgust.

"Uh, Debbie," said Marianne. "About Atlantis Park . . . I don't want you to go there alone, while your father and I are out filming."

"WHAT?!" Debbie exploded.

"You let Eliza wander the Serengeti with nothing but a monkey and a wildboy," Debbie ranted, "but I can't go to an *amusement park?!*"

"Honey, that park is as big as a city," said Marianne. "You haven't been around crowded places for a long time. You're not used to the things that can happen."

"Your mother's right, pumpkin," said Nigel.

"Look, I'll take you to Atlantis tomorrow,"

promised Marianne.

Debbie stomped away, grumbling, "Oh, yeah, it'll be easy to make friends with my *mother* holding my hand!"

Chapter 2
A Missing Mother

With her parents off filming and Debbie pouting in the Commvee, Eliza decided to go snorkeling. "Come on, Darwin!" she called.

"I am NOT being eaten by a crocodile, thank you very much!" Darwin answered.

Hyacinth nodded. "We like to swim near the outflow pipes of the Atlantis Park because the water is warm," she said. "But some humans were boat racing there yesterday. We got separated from our mother."

"The park has an animal rescue facility," Eliza told the manatees. "If your mama was injured, I bet they found her. I'll check it out. You stay here, okay?"

As Eliza swam back to the Commvee, Hydrilla called, "Mama's easy to spot! She has a white streak on her head from when a boat hit her last year!"

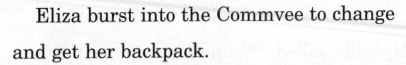

Eliza burst into the Commvee to change
and get her backpack.

"Where are you going?" Debbie demanded.

"Uh . . . Atlantis Park," Eliza confessed.

"WHAT?" Debbie cried. "If I can't go, what
makes you think *you* can?"

"Because I have to," said Eliza. "It's really important, okay? Please don't tell Mom and Dad."

Debbie grinned and grabbed her purse. "Gee, I'd better go with you," she said. "You shouldn't go alone."

Eliza sighed. "Whatever. Don't forget Donnie."

Chapter 3
Searching Atlantis

Once at Atlantis Park, Debbie went to find some "cool kids" to hang with, grudgingly taking Donnie with her.

Eliza checked the park map. "This way to the Aquatic Emergency Treatment Center," she told Darwin. "And straighten your hat."

Eliza soon found Hyacinth and Hydrilla's mother swimming in an isolation tank. "Don't worry," Eliza told the sea cow. "We're here to help!"

Eliza found the office and opened the door. "Excuse me," she blurted, "but I recognize that manatee cow outside. I've found her pups!"

Three veterinarians turned to face Eliza. "You found them?" asked one, obviously pleased.

"Wait," said another vet. "How do you know they're *her* pups?"

"Now you've done it!" Darwin whispered. "You can't tell them you can *talk* to manatees!"

"Oh, keep your skirt on," Eliza whispered back.

Darwin frowned. "Very funny."

"I was watching the manatees yesterday when some boat racers went by," Eliza explained. "When the water settled, they were gone. But I spotted the babies by the Commvee this morning."

"Commvee?" repeated the vet. "*Nigel Thornberry's* Commvee?"

"Yeah," said Eliza. "I'm Eliza Thornberry."

"Wow!" the vet said. "I'm a fan of your dad's show!"

"Those boat racers were caught by the Coast Guard," said another vet. "They said they'd scared some manatees. But when we looked, we only found the mother."

"Was she hurt?" Eliza asked.

"Just dazed," the vet assured her. "She's fine now."

"Then come on!" said Eliza. "I'll take you to the pups!" Then she remembered Debbie and Donnie. "Oh, I'd better find my sister first. I'll be right back!"

Chapter 4
Debbie's New Friend

Debbie was having a blast, even with
Donnie hanging around. She had met a cute
guy named Chris, who was so sweet that
she didn't even mind when he spilled
ketchup on her.

But suddenly someone darted by and
snatched Debbie's purse. "HEY!" she
squealed in surprise. "Chris, move! I can't
see . . . !"

Debbie started to run after the thief.
"You are so busted!" she yelled. "I've
outraced dingoes, you know!"

But Chris held her back. "No, Debbie!"
he said. "It's too dangerous!"

"Then we have to report this!" Debbie said.

"Without a description, the cops can't catch the guy," Chris said reasonably. "Debbie, this sort of thing happens all the time."

"Great," said Debbie. "Here comes my sister."

"Which one's your sister?" asked Chris.

Debbie just looked at him blankly.

Eliza saw Debbie's expression. "What happened?"

"Somebody took my purse," Debbie growled.

Eliza gasped. "Did you see who?"

"No," Debbie admitted, then added, "Oh, Eliza, this is Chris. Chris, this is Eliza and . . ." She winced at Darwin. "And . . . Babs."

Eliza nodded to Chris, then asked, "Did you report it?"

Debbie shrugged. "Chris says it happens all the time."

"All the more reason to report it!" Eliza told Chris sharply. "You would if it was *your* money!"

Debbie blinked. "Yeah," she said thoughtfully. "I bet you would . . ."

Suddenly Debbie's face grew pale. "You know, *you* blocked my view of the thief," she said. "And *you* stopped me from going after him or reporting it. Now that I think about it, *you* spilled the ketchup on me—*on purpose!*"

"You're in with him!" Debbie realized. *"You're a thief, too!"*

Chris tried to run, but Donnie and Darwin weren't about to let him escape.

"You like purses, do you?" Darwin muttered. "Then, take THIS!" He whacked Chris with his purse.

Eliza grabbed the ketchup bottle. "Don't
move," she warned Chris, "or I'll squirt!"

Just then a park security officer hurried
up. "We caught a kid with this," he said,
holding up a purse. "Is it yours?"

Debbie nodded, embarrassed. "Yeah. Thanks."

Chapter 5
Reunited

Later at the Commvee, Eliza and Darwin
watched as the mama manatee was
reunited with her pups.

51

After the rescue boat left, Eliza and Darwin
climbed down to water level.

"Thank you, Eliza," said the mama manatee.
"Because of you, my family is together again."

"Glad I could help," said Eliza, waving
good-bye.

When Eliza entered the Commvee, she found Debbie scrubbing the ketchup stain out of her blouse.

"I'm such a fool," Debbie moaned.

"Mom was right. I'm so used to living in the wilderness that I can dodge a rhino without batting an eye," Debbie went on. "But I fall for an obvious con job!"

"Hey, every environment has its dangers," said Eliza. "Some animals are dangerous and some aren't, just like some people are honest and some aren't. You're just more used to one than the other."

"But you got your purse back, the thieves were caught, and no one got hurt," Eliza continued. "And you figured it all out."

Debbie grinned. "Yeah, I did, didn't I?"

Debbie gave her sister a hug. "You're a dweeb, Eliza," she said, "but you're an okay dweeb."

Eliza giggled. "Gee, thanks."

Later that evening, Eliza's parents returned. "Oh, I could spend days mucking around in those lovely swamps!" said Nigel, sighing. "How about tomorrow, Marianne?"

"Sorry, Nigel," said Marianne. "But I promised Debbie a day at Atlantis Park." She smiled at Debbie.

"Well, actually, Mom, I've changed my mind. How about we go here instead?" Debbie asked, holding up a brochure for

Eco-Everglades Airboat Tours. Then Debbie winked at Eliza. "I mean, why go to a park *about* the Everglades when we have the *real* Everglades right here?"